There are many individuals who participated in this exciting project. Perhaps those that inspired and motivated us most are our beloved animals. As the backbone of our career and life, they are our 'bringers of joy'.

To all of our wonderful family and friends who have supported us from the beginning, thank you very much for always believing in us.

To our dedicated fans, we thank you for coming to our shows and becoming collectors of our book series. The adventure has just begun; get those Jungle Journals ready!

We are very fortunate to have the editing duo of Anne and Jim Shute from Guelph, Ontario, on the team. We would like to thank them for being encouraging, helpful and always loving.

Many thanks to our creative and artistic dream team of Rob Davie and Amy Sheppard. Rob's artwork and illustrations capture the admiration of all ages. He is truly gifted. Amy's ability to transform text and image into art is extraordinary. Thank you both for sharing your abilities with the Great Green Adventure Series.

The Read-A-Long CD has become the highlight for many 'Greeners' and parents alike. The CD is a joyful combination of comical character voices, original toe-tapping music and creative sound effects.

We would like to thank those directly involved with its production: Shawn Healey as Safari Jeff, Tanya Goral as Shannon, Adam MacGilvary as Dr. Evergreen, Jason Shute as Shaman Nano, Kofi Howarth Shute as Jose, Jeffrey McKay as Father Time, Huntzman and El Machismo, Shannon Kavanagh as Narrator.

We thank Jeremy Shute for writing the music, creating the sound effects, arranging the mix and for being an all around great help. Final productions were made in Guelph, Ontario, at Monastereo Recording Studio.

We would like to thank Tycho and Tia with Kigloo Media for creating the fantastically popular www.greatgreenadventure.com. This website has a life of its own; great work T's!

We dedicate this book to our mothers and fathers, Lynda Halstead, Paul Kavanagh, Brian And Bernice McKay, our number one supporters in good times and bad. This series would not have succeeded without their ongoing love, support, encouragement and guidance.

All the best,
Shannon and Jeff

Welcome to the Adventure!
Violet,

Safari Jeff

CROCTALK Publishing ISBN 0-9734409-1-0

Artwork & Illustrations © Robert Davie

Photos © Greg Gerla Photography

Text © Shannon Kavanagh

Research and Development: Jeffrey McKay

Editors: Anne and Jim Shute

Book Design:
Deep Blue Design
www.deepbluedesign.ca

Sponsor:
Tilley Endurables
www.tilley.com

The Adventure continues at
www.greatgreenadventure.com

Collect all 7 books for the complete global experience!
AFRICA • SOUTH AMERICA • ANTARCTICA
AUSTRALIA • ASIA • EUROPE • NORTH AMERICA

Printed in Canada on recycled paper ♻

Limited Edition

(The great green adventure series)
Written by Shannon Kavanagh, illustrated by Rob Davie.

ISBN 0-9734409-1-0

Safari Jeff and Shannon visit South America

THE GREAT GREEN ADVENTURE SERIES - BOOK 2

Welcome to the second book in the Great Green Adventure series Safari Jeff and Shannon Visit South America.

We're very happy you've decided to join our team of adventurers.

This exciting book will help you become a travel and wildlife enthusiast.

It's simple to get involved. Collect information, photos and sketches in your JUNGLE JOURNAL. Fill it up by writing down facts, pasting photos or sketching things you like or that interest you, such as animals, the planet, dinosaurs or anything at all!

Gather your JUNGLE JOURNAL content from books, the Internet, television and your own experiences. Once you've filled in the pages, share your facts with others. The more people learn and understand about nature, the more they will want to conserve it.

Thank you for joining the Great Green Adventure. Our planet needs you.

Good luck on this exciting journey! Here's to a 'Greener" future!

Your friends,

Safari Jeff, Shannon, Dr. Evergreen, Father Time and Huntzman

On a beautiful sunny day in East Africa,

a team of adventure seekers
prepare themselves for an exciting journey to a yet
unknown continent.

Dr. Evergreen is a tiny scientist who leads this magical tour in his air balloon.
He is joined by a crew of inquisitive naturalists and a few of their amazing animal friends.

Together they are on a quest called the Great Green Adventure. They plan to collect interesting photos and facts about animals, plants, people and places. Their goal is to fill their Jungle Journals with fascinating information that they can share with others. Dr. Evergreen taught the team that to become a naturalist, you must share what you know with others. The Great Green Adventurers or, as Dr. Evergreen calls them, the "Greeners", had just completed a spectacular visit to Africa. The travellers were eager for their next venture, this time to discover nature's mysteries in another part of the blue planet.

While Jeff stuffed his pack with essentials, Shannon eagerly waited beside the balloon and announced "This is excitement; who knows were we might end up? South America is a huge continent! I want to see crocodiles. I'm ready, so can we go now?" She paced back and forth anxiously while wearing her pack and holding her Jungle Journal. Jeff laughed, shook his head and chuckled "Settle down, trail blazer! I'm excited, too, but we'll have to get there first. Anyway, Dr. Evergreen hasn't even found all of his gear yet."

While grumbling to himself, Dr. Evergreen looked around impatiently for his trusty brass telescope. As a practiced traveller, he never lifts off without all of his essential adventure gear, such as a compass, water flask, flashlight, camera and Jungle Journal.

With an unsettled look on his face, Dr. Evergreen scratched his bristly white beard, then hollered over to Jeff,

"Have you seen my hoo-ja-ma-doodle?"

2

Jeff paused for a moment with a confused look on his face and replied, "You are looking for your what?"

The frustrated scientist began to bend and twist his durable Tilley hat, then blurted, "You know, my whatchamacallit!"

Giggling to herself, Shannon held up Dr. Evergreen's precious telescope and said, "Look! here is your thingamabob!"

They paused, smiling at each other, then burst into laughter at how silly they all sounded. In good spirits they laughed and joked, made goofy sounds and made up funny words while loading the balloon with adventure gear.

Just then, Dr. Evergreen bounced to his tiny feet and appeared to be listening to something far off in the distance. He cupped his ear, then licked his thumb and held it above his head as far as he could reach and gasped, "Yup! That's the one. Get into the balloon. The wind is headed west and it's our ride, so load up quickly!"

"He cupped his ear, then licked his thumb"

The team helped to load the heavy tortoise into his balloon, then jumped into their balloon and braced themselves for gust off.

As predicted by Dr. Evergreen, a sudden wind began swirling under and around the balloon, carrying it upwards into the blue sky.

"Yahoo!" screeched Huntzman the hawk. "Off to another mystery continent on the Great Green Adventure. This one is going to be a whirlwind of fun; I can feel it in my feathers!" The hawk stretched his wings and glided away from the balloon to help navigate wind currents for the journey ahead. Huntzman joined the team as a scout and guardian; with vision 10 times sharper than that of a human, he was a valuable team member.

Father Time, the tortoise, seems to accompany Jeff and Shannon for any and all of their many adventures. He assured the team that if he joined them, he would be a great resource in helping them complete their Jungle Journals because of his encyclopedic knowledge of nature.

Each of the adventure seekers had special qualities, and all of them together made a great team.

As the balloon travelled across the Atlantic along the equator, they reminisced about the experiences they had shared in Africa, the wonderful people they had met there and the beautiful animals they had photographed.

Welcome to Venezuela!

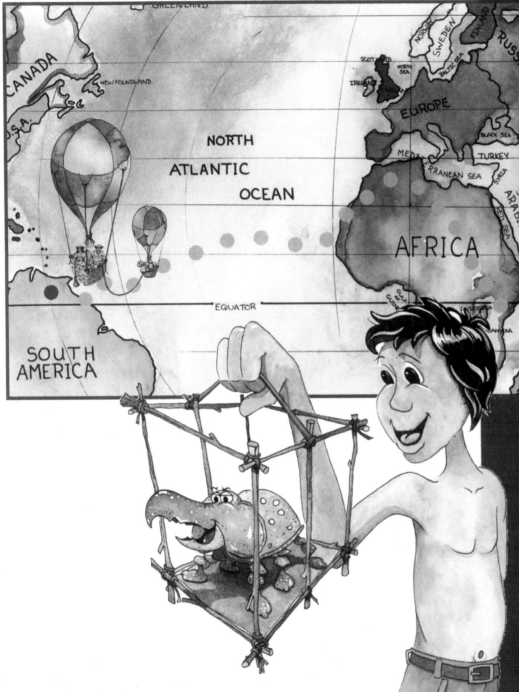

Their travels across the ocean were much faster this time, as they were lucky to catch the perfect wind currents which took them directly to the very top of South America, beautiful Venezuela. Huntzman soared by the balloon at top speed and screeched, "Follow me Greeners! I've got a great landing spot down there in that sugarcane field." He tucked his wings and dove towards the earth's surface like a bolt of lightning. As the balloon descended from the sky, the team noticed a small house with wooden walls, a rusted tin roof and a family watching them curiously.

As they neared the ground, a young boy ran towards them carrying a small cage made of twine and sticks. He greeted the floating strangers with a big smile and said "Bienvenidos (welcome); my name is Jose and this is my pet beetle El Machismo. Welcome to Venezuela!" The team jumped out of the balloon and greeted the boy, then met Humberto, his father, and Nena, his mother. They were very friendly and invited the team to stay for dinner.

They had ayote(squash) soup and fried plantain for dinner and as they dined, unusual sneezing and sniffling sounds were coming from around the kitchen. Dr. Evergreen slid his chair back and caught a glimpse of a young tapir hiding below the counter. When she saw Dr. Evergreen she began to sneeze uncontrollably, spraying her snout juice all over the kitchen. "What's wrong with the wee creature? She seems scared", observed Dr. Evergreen.

Humberto explained how they recently had a huge storm and their garden was completely washed out. When the family came outside after the flood, this young tapir was hiding behind the house. She had been separated from her family and was all alone.

They had been trying to care for her but all she would eat or drink was coconut milk, so Jose lovingly named her Pipa which means coconut in Spanish. Jose explained that Pipa would sneeze this way when she was nervous, spraying everyone with her swaying snout.

Jeff attempted to call the tapir over and made a suggestion to the group, "We could help the family rebuild their garden and with all of us here it wouldn't take any time at all." Shannon offered Pipa some coconut milk out of her hat and said, "We could help Pipa find her family, too. I bet they're looking for her along the river and she could come with us."

Dr. Evergreen smiled at his team of adventurers and said, "I couldn't have asked for a nicer group of Greeners. Good for you; helping others is important. All right then, full steam ahead!"

The team began to clean, rake and seed the damaged garden for their new friends. Dr. Evergreen somehow managed to get a caterpillar in his beard; he always seemed to have something stuck in it.

Pipa

Father Time began eating some of the old garden plants that Humberto was planning on burning in the fire pit and with a mouth full of greens he gargled, "You call this garbage? This is a heavenly salad buffet of delights. Pass it over. Waste not, want not!"

The team made short work of the family's garden and then it was back to planning the rest of the adventure. Humberto was very grateful for the efforts of these strangers, who were now amigos(friends). He insisted on giving them a traditional dugout canoe as a token of appreciation.

The team gathered their belongings and Nena packed them a few snacks for their journey ahead. Shannon was nervous about the river journey and asked, "Do you think we might need a guide to navigate us through the rivers safely?"

Jeff and Dr. Evergreen looked at each other in agreement and then Jeff said, "It would be a good idea but where would we find a river guide around here?"

"Look no more, my friends! I am El Machismo"

At that moment, Jose's beetle kicked open his cage door, leaped to the ground and scurried towards Dr. Evergreen while clanging his front pincers together like cymbals to get everyone's attention. Then the armour-plated beetle stopped, lifted himself onto two hind legs, wobbled about for a second, then announced deeply and confidently, "Look no more, my friends! I am El Machismo, strong like a bull and swift like a spider. I will take you down the river and protect you from the crocodiles. I call this my servicio especial (special service). Trust me amigos (friends), I will guide you; I know which rivers to follow to get you to Machu Picchu, where the mountains are tall and the grasses are green."

The Greeners gazed at each other completely surprised at the courage of this adventurous beetle, then gladly accepted his offer.

Father Time smacked his jaws together, released a loud burst of air through his nostrils, and then groaned, "Yes, sounds just great. Now let's get a move on, shall we?

I can already taste the luscious grasses and tasty flowers. Huntzman, shine up those feathers, my boy. It's lift-off to the land of plenty."

With the strength of Huntzman's talons, wings, and a helpful gust of air, the balloon left the earth and the two were up and away. They were destined for the beautiful country of Peru, along the Pacific Ocean on the west coast of South America. It was in the ancient ruins of Machu Picchu where the team planned to reunite at the balloon for their next Great Green Adventure.

The Greeners felt very excited, nervous and anxious all at the same time. They knew that this journey would be filled with amazing discoveries. However, they also knew of the potential dangers that lay ahead and this made them all a bit worried.

Once they reached the river, El Machismo scurried to the bow of the boat to navigate and guide. Pipa would trail behind as tapirs are fantastic swimmers, while Jeff and Shannon steered with bamboo poles.

Dr. Evergreen strategically placed himself in mid-canoe, as this would be the perfect location for him to sketch in his Jungle Journal undisturbed by the navigators. He placed his gear around his feet to stabilize himself then said, "I sketch well in a canoe; for some reason I'm always inspired by the gracefulness of a canoe through water. These dimly lit rivers are no place to take photos, so you'll have to sharpen your pencils, folks; we'll be sketching from here on."

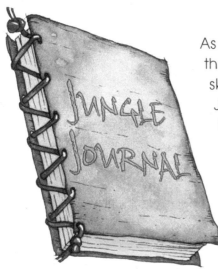

As they drifted silently down the river, Dr. Evergreen sketched creatures in his Jungle Journal while El Machismo pointed out all kinds of animals in the trees, in the water and on land. They passed colourful tree frogs and tree boas and a friendly arrowana fish travelled alongside the canoe, making spectacular leaps into the air snatching insects from leaves and branches. El Machismo explained that the male arrowana will carry its young in its mouth for months, protecting them from predators and during that time he will not eat for fear of leaving the babies.

El Machismo also explained how many animals use camouflage to help protect themselves from predators; "It is the best defense, my friends. Hunters cannot eat you if they cannot see you", he puffed.

They had been travelling safely for many hours when Jeff noticed that the current had quickened and that they were approaching a sharp bend in the river.

Spoonbill

This bird uses its spooned beak by weaving or waving from side to side through the water. Sensitive nerve endings allow the bird to feel when its beak comes in contact with food and it shuts its strainer. It munches on small fish, shellfish, insects, shrimp and other amphipods. It has been known to feed in both salt and fresh water. It maintains its pink colour through the food it eats.

Capybara

The capybara is the largest rodent in the world, and weighs up to 73 kilograms. It lives in tall grasslands that border rivers, streams and lakes in tropical South America and Panama. Its legs are fairly short, its toes are webbed and it has hoof-like claws. Jaguars and cougars are the main enemies of this gentle creature but it is also preyed upon by large snakes, crocodilians and eagles.

TIPS:

While watching your favourite nature show, take notes of interesting facts, like "some fish communicate by making sounds" or "baby lions cubs are born with spots".

Take photographs and create sketches to accompany your journal information.

Always carry a pencil and paper while hiking, camping or travelling. These are great opportunities to discover plants and wildlife, and to take notes!

As the river narrowed, it propelled the canoe forward, leaving Pipa behind struggling and sneezing in the swirling, bubbling water. The canoe quickly rounded the corner and they all gasped to see a barricade of hungry crocodiles with their mouths open, catching fish in the rapids.

The adventure team was headed directly towards the wall of snarling teeth, when El Machismo instructed Jeff to throw a rope around an oncoming tree branch. Almost in the same moment, the beetle lunged off the side of the canoe, caught Pipa by the ear with this mighty pincer, held on tightly while Jeff bravely pulled them towards the shore with all his strength.

The team dragged themselves onto dry land; they were completely drenched from the splashing water but safe from the carnivorous crocodiles. They took a deep breath, shook off the water and the fright and then began a search for any lost gear.

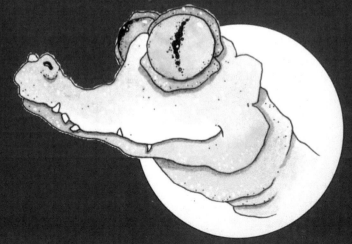

While searching, Shannon heard some rustling noises coming from the forest, and then spied two black eyes peering through a bush. Pipa bounded to her hooves and ran gleefully towards the stranger in the bush, knowing that it was another tapir.

The two tapirs rejoiced to be in each other's company, skipped around for a moment, then headed towards the forest together. Pipa looked back at the Greeners, batting her long eyelashes lovingly, and then skipped off into the wilderness with her new companion.

"See", Dr. Evergreen sniffled, "That's the way to do it. Way to go, team! Pipa found her way and we escaped becoming crocodile food. It's a good day for adventure."

Alerted by all the commotion, three Amazonians appeared out of the bush with frowns on their faces and sharp spears in their hands. The cautious Dr. Evergreen slowly stepped out of the canoe, raised his hands, lowered his head and said "Shaman Nano?" The skeptical Yanomami men stared intently at the Greeners, whistled loudly, then motioned for Dr. Evergreen to step forward and stop.

Out of the forest shuffled a small man decorated in a feathered headdress, painted face and bone necklaces. He was the shaman, a doctor of the rainforest who uses plants to heal the sick.

Nano the Shaman smiled at Dr. Evergreen then said, "Nabe (non-Indian) Evergreen, you must be here for some of my adventure foot rub you love so much." Dr. Evergreen slapped his hands together then exclaimed. "Well, I'll be jiggered! It's my good friend Nano the Shaman. I'd love some of your magic mixes and perhaps a remedy for my itchy face, too. I had a few caterpillars nest in my beard on this voyage and it's been irritating me ever since."

The two old friends laughed and rubbed their foreheads together in greeting, then turned towards the village. The shaman looked at his friend's beard and said, "I've got just the flower for that problem. Come with me to my yano(tepee) but your friends must remain here. They are strangers in our village and must receive the chief's approval before entering."

"No problemo for me, man", gulped the quivering beetle. "I'll stay right here in the boat. The Yanomami will eat most animals and beetle is not on the menu tonight, thank you very much!" he puffed.

The Greeners stayed behind on shore, guarded by the Amazonians, and they used the time off to continue sketching in their Jungle Journals. They observed animals, had a nap in the sun, ate some fresh fruit and waited for Dr. Evergreen to return with his rainforest remedies.

Jeff and Shannon were just about to put their Journals away when an enormous Harpy eagle gracefully landed on a rock in the middle of the river to catch some afternoon sunshine. They pulled out their pencils and began to sketch the beautiful bird, feather by feather. The bird seemed to pose for them as they captured the details of the spectacular creature.

Some noise coming from the forest startled the eagle and as he took off, Dr. Evergreen emerged with an armful of gifts from Nano.

They gave each other a customary farewell, then Nano held Dr. Evergreen by the cheeks and said, "You are a true waithiri (giver of gifts) my friend. I wish that you never change."

Nano smiled at the eavesdropping Greeners and said, "To be a true waithiri, you must give as well as you get. Nabe Evergreen will always be my friend."

Eager to continue on their surprising adventure down the amazing Amazon River, the team slowly pushed off so as not to startle the feeding crocodiles.

it, they could see a long winding trail in the tall grass where Father Time had eaten through. "He's been munching since we got here. Not sure how we're going to lift off with all the weight he's packed on!", Huntzman mumbled.

El Machismo continued to share fascinating information with the team for their Jungle Journals, such as how the Amazon River carries 25% of the earth's water and how one single Amazonian tree can nurture over 2000 species of plants and animals.

As the team neared their destination in Peru, they heard a familiar sound coming from the sky above, a squawking sound that could only be everyone's favourite bird,

Huntzman the hawk.

"Squawk! Great to see you all. I thought you'd got lost. Right this way, mes amigos (my friends)" Huntzman guided the team towards the mountain and as they approached

The Greeners were amazed by the magnitude and beauty of Machu Picchu. It was a memorable moment to be in such an ancient and spiritual place.

The Great Green Adventure team compiled some fantastic content for their Jungle Journals. Jeff and Shannon were already busy sharing information and adding finishing touches to the sketches they had begun.

Dr. Evergreen was glowing with enthusiasm as he held the bamboo pole above his head and blurted, "This is why I love my life! Adventure with new people, in new places, with so much to see, learn and do. How could we possibly top this Great Green Adventure?" He stroked his beard with a devilish grin then said, " Perhaps with a bit of snow!"

The Greeners cheered and said, "Antarctica?! That will be awesome!" The team set up camp and began planning and mapping for their future journey to the land of ice.

The End

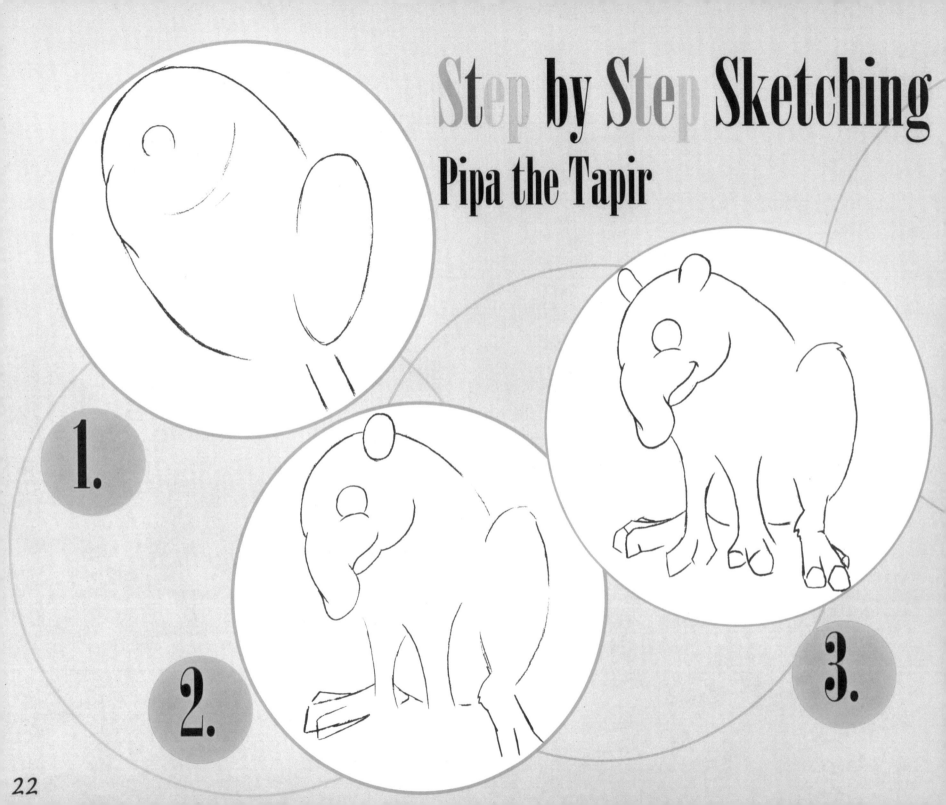

Step by Step Sketching
Pipa the Tapir

1.

2.

3.

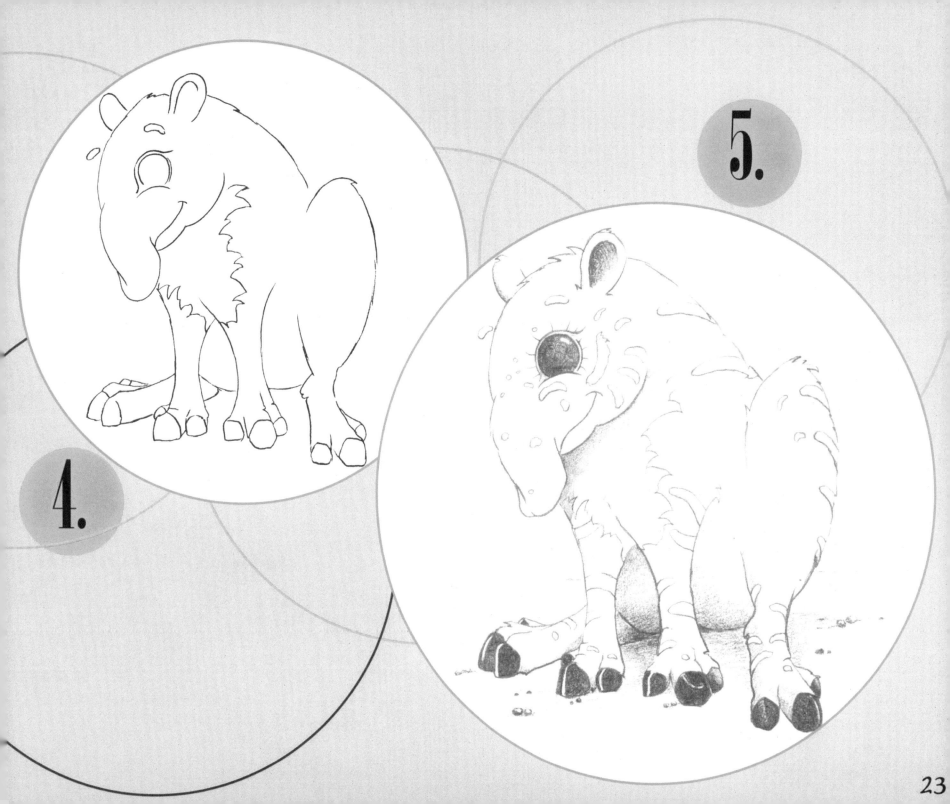

4.

5.

23

YOU BE THE ARTIST!

Pipa the Tapir

Hoatzin

The Hoatzin is a living bird that shows similarities to the first known bird, Archaeopteryx. One of the more interesting and ancient characteristics is the presence of claws on the wings. The young use these claws to clamber among the branches near the nest, much the way its ancestors did millions of years ago. The Hoatzin is placed in a family or order of birds all by itself.

HOATZIN "BRAZIL"

Hercules Beetle

Sloth

On the ground and in the trees, two-toed sloths move very slowly but are surprisingly good swimmers. Their ancestor, the giant sloth, which lived before the last ice age, reached the size of the modern elephant.

The Hercules Beetle can grow up to 11cm in length. It has huge sword-shaped horns that can be 6cm to 10cm long. It comes out at night to feed on sap and is found in lush tropical rainforests near the equator.

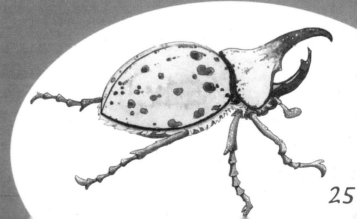

25

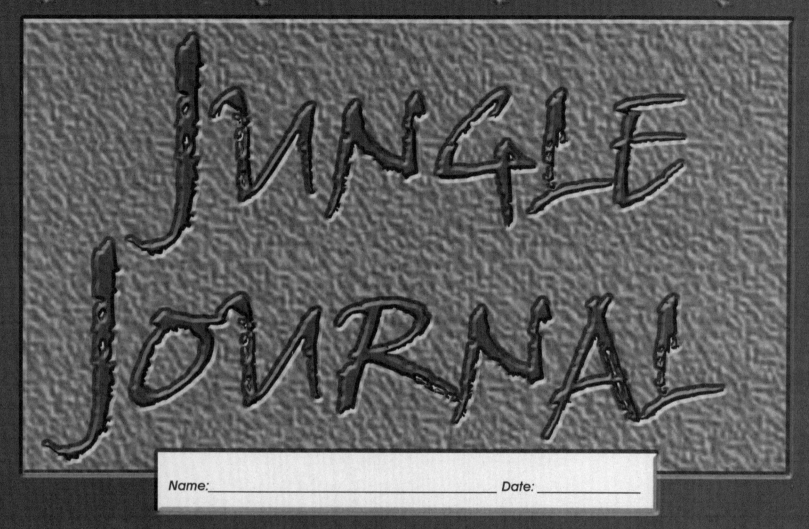

JUNGLE JOURNAL

Name:_____ Date: _____

Now is your chance to become a 'Greener' on the Great Green Adventure.

Be sure to check off your Rainforest Gear List and put your name in your official *Jungle Journal* before you start the adventure.
We've started you off with some facts and photos. Now it's up to you to collect your own information,
photos and sketches to fill up your Journal.

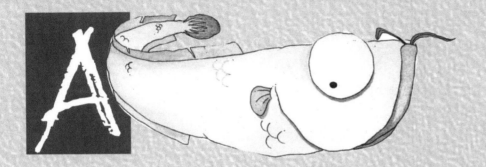

Arrowana

The Arrowana is often called the "Dragon Fish"
because it has a body covered with big, shiny
scales. It is omnivorous, feeding on fish at
the surface or leaping from the water to catch
large insects resting on tree branches.

Colombia Boa

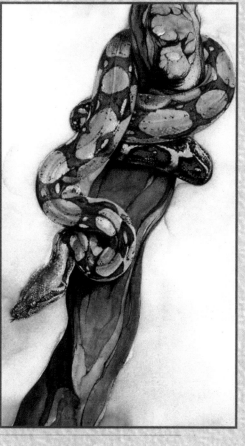

The Colombian boas are

often kept as pets,

as they become very

docile and they eat any

visiting rodents

Crocodile

Crocodiles have a four-chambered heart (like humans), as well as three sets of eyelids and two sets of muscles. Crocodiles replace teeth whenever necessary and they never stop growing.

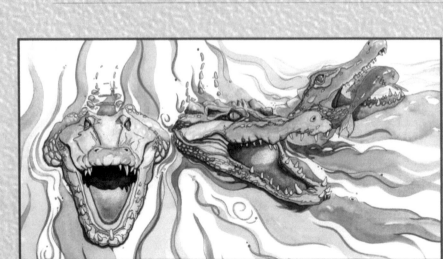

Digits

Fingers on the hand are the digits.

The thumb can rotate 90 degrees, whereas the

fingers can only rotate 45 degrees. Having

opposable thumbs enables humans to grasp and

hold objects.

Harpy Eagle

Harpy Eagles will bring fresh green twigs to the nest. This helps to fumigate against insects and parasites.

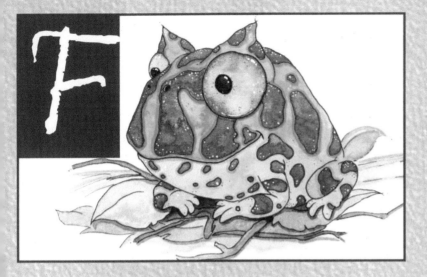

Horned **Frog**

Neonate horned frogs are highly carnivorous when growing but are also known to be cannibalistic and will eat their sibling neonates. As adults, the horned frogs will swallow prey up to their own body size, feeding on frogs, lizards, mice, and large insects.

Guanacos

Guanacos are related to camels, as are vicunas, llamas and alpacas. One difference is that guanacos live in South America while camels are found in Africa and Asia. Guanacos live high in the Andes mountains—up to 3,962 metres above sea level. They also inhabit the lower plateaus, plains, and coastlines of Peru, Chile, and Argentina.

Hoatzin

HOATZIN
BRAZIL

The Hoatzin is a living bird that shows similarities

to the first known bird, Archaeopteryx. One of

the more interesting and ancient characteristics is

the presence of claws on the wings. The

Hoatzin is placed in a family or order of birds

all by itself.

Iguana

Green iguanas have good

senses of hearing, smell and superb vision. These

sturdy creatures can fall 12 to 15 metres to the

ground, unharmed. Both male and female iguanas

can store fat under their jaws for times of food

and water shortages.

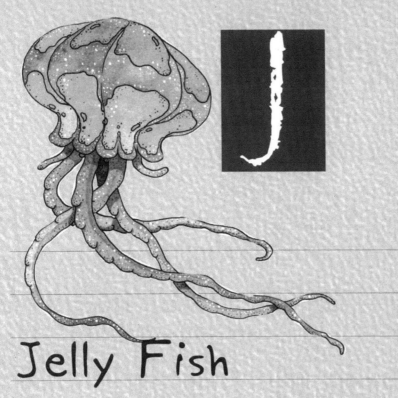

Kinkajou

The kinkajou is known as the "night walker". It

feeds mainly on fruit and insects among the upper

canopy of tropical rainforests. Kinkajous are

extremely agile and fast in the treetops. It has

a prehensile tail used to balance and hold on to

tree branches.

Jelly Fish

The symmetry (shape) of the jellyfish allows it to

respond to food or danger from any direction.

Instead of a brain, it possesses a nervous system

with receptors that detect light and odour.

Lehmann's Tree Frog

This Colombian frog reaches 36mm in length. Males attract females with a series of calls, coaxing the female to lay eggs. The male then fertilizes and protects the eggs to insure their survival. Tadpoles are usually cannibalistic, so the male separates each egg to a different site to develop safely.

Macaw

Macaws have a broad and fleshy tongue which is strengthened by a horny layer under the tip. The beak and tongue together make an excellent tool for cracking seeds and digging holes. The beak is also used as a third hand while climbing. Their feet (two toes forward, two back) also give them excellent climbing ability.

N Neon Tetra

These fish are native to the Peruvian Amazon

where they live in shaded jungle waters. They

are brightly coloured so that they can find each

other in the dark waters.

O Ocelot

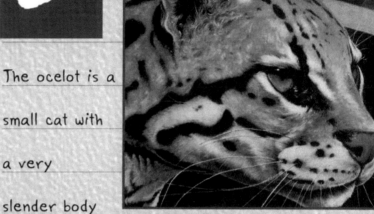

The ocelot is a

small cat with

a very

slender body

that can measure up to 1.2 metres. It hunts

mostly at night for rabbits, rodents, reptiles and

the occasional small deer. The ocelot is a great

swimmer and sleeps in the lower branches of

trees in its habitat.

Peru

Peru's indigenous people speak

Quechua and live in the Andes.

In the 12th century the

Quecha-speaking Inca built a fortress called

Machu Picchu.

Quills

Porcupine quills are a fantastic defense against most predators. However, fishers and mountain lions eat porcupines with little trouble. Porcupines eat bark high in the trees during the winter then shift to plants on the ground in the summer.

Rainforest

More than 50 percent of the earth's species live in the rainforest. At least 25 percent of all modern healing drugs originally came from the rainforest. Many of the foods we eat today, such as chocolate, coffee, sugar, and vanilla, came from the rainforest.

Spoonbill

It maintains its pink

colour through the food

it eats.

Tapir

The South American tapir

is the smallest of four

species found on the planet,

weighing in at 181 kilograms.

Baby tapirs gain about .45 kilograms per day for

the first year of life. Tapirs swim very well and

are stealthy runners, much like their

relatives the horse and rhinoceros.

U-V Ray

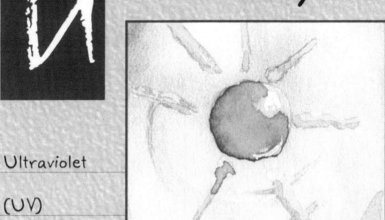

Ultraviolet

(UV)

radiation

consists of invisible rays from the sun.

The three bands of UV light are: UVA, UVB

and UVC. UVC rays are of little concern as

they are absorbed by the upper atmosphere.

However, sunglasses and sunscreen are essential

for UVA protection.

Vampire Bat

The vampire bat feeds exclusively on the blood of

birds and mammals. A vampire bat finds its prey

with echolocation, smell and sound. A bat is a

flying mammal.

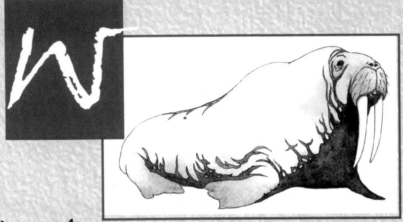

Walrus

A walrus can dive up to 121 metres to retrieve its food; it can eat 4000 clams in one feeding. The walrus has an air sac in its neck which allows it to sleep with its head held up out of the water.

Xenarthra

(scientific classification for sloth)

On the ground and in the trees, two-toed sloths move very slowly but are surprisingly good swimmers. Their ancestor, the giant sloth, which lived before the last ice age, reached the size of the modern elephant.

Yanomami

The Yanomami are an indigenous people living in the tropical

rainforests of Southern Venezuela and Northern Brazil. The approximately 20,000 Yanomami alive today are considered to be an endangered people. Yanomami means "human being".

Zygodactyls

A zygodactyl is a bird with four toes, two pointing forward and two pointing backward. The macaw is a zygodactyl, giving it the ability to grasp a tree branch firmly. Tendons in its ankle lock when it is asleep, preventing the bird from falling.

About the Artist

Rob Davie is from the small town of Tottenham, Ontario. It is here where he spent the first seven years of his life making pets out of creatures like snapping turtles and June bugs.

Rob has always been interested in why animals are the way they are. Constantly observing their movement, colour, shape, texture, etc. Inevitably, his interests expanded to studying more exotic creatures and eventually they became the main subject of his artwork.

Rob has been residing in Calgary, Alberta since 1977. He still keeps some exotic pets and when time permits he enjoys educating children, sharing his knowledge of animals and teaching them to respect and appreciate the living things around us.

Rob graduated from the Alberta College of Art and Design in 1994 majoring in Visual Communications, including an additional year as a drawing major. Working with a variety of media including pencil, watercolor and acrylics, Rob's love of animals becomes quite apparent in all of his work.

It is his hope that his pieces influence viewers to take the time to truly appreciate the beauty of things that most of us take for granted.

Rob would like to dedicate the artwork in this book to his mother, Noreen.

She will be forever missed.